ORANGE

LOVE

GLUE

Emily's Idea

Sounds True
Boulder, CO 80306

Text © 2020 Christine Evans

Illustrations © 2020 Marta Álvarez Miguéns

Published 2020

Book design by Ranée Kahler

Printed in South Korea

Library of Congress Cataloging-in-Publication Data

Names: Evans, Christine (Christine N.), author. | Álvarez Miguéns, Marta,
  1976- illustrator.
Title: Emily's idea / by Christine Evans ; illustrated by Marta Alvarez
  Miguens.
Description: Boulder, CO : Sounds True, 2020. | Summary: Emily makes a
  chain of paper dolls, and her creation catches on in her classroom and
  spreads across town and throughout the world. Includes instructions for
  making a chain of paper dolls.
Identifiers: LCCN 2019024436 (print) | LCCN 2019024437 (ebook) |
  ISBN 9781683644163 (hardback) | ISBN 9781683644170 (ebook)
Subjects: CYAC: Paper work--Fiction. | Sharing--Fiction.
Classification: LCC PZ7.1.E8594 Em 2020 (print) | LCC PZ7.1.E8594
  (ebook) | DDC [E]--dc23
LC record available at https://lccn.loc.gov/2019024436
LC ebook record available at https://lccn.loc.gov/2019024437

10 9 8 7 6 5 4 3 2 1

Emily's Idea

sounds true
BOULDER, COLORADO

Written by Christine Evans • Illustrated by Marta Álvarez Miguéns

Emily's idea started small. Many beautiful ideas do.
She folded, doodled, and snipped.

But also, like many ideas, Emily's small idea grew.
Until her room was alive with pattern and color.

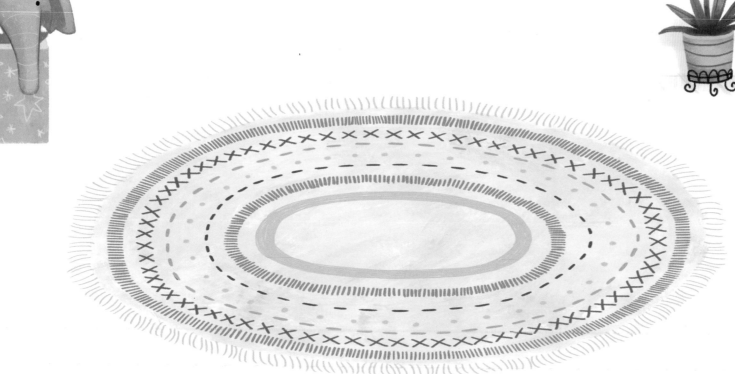

On share day, Emily's paper dolls inspired Ms. Tate and room 6B.
So everyone folded, doodled, and snipped. Each doll was
different, but the same.

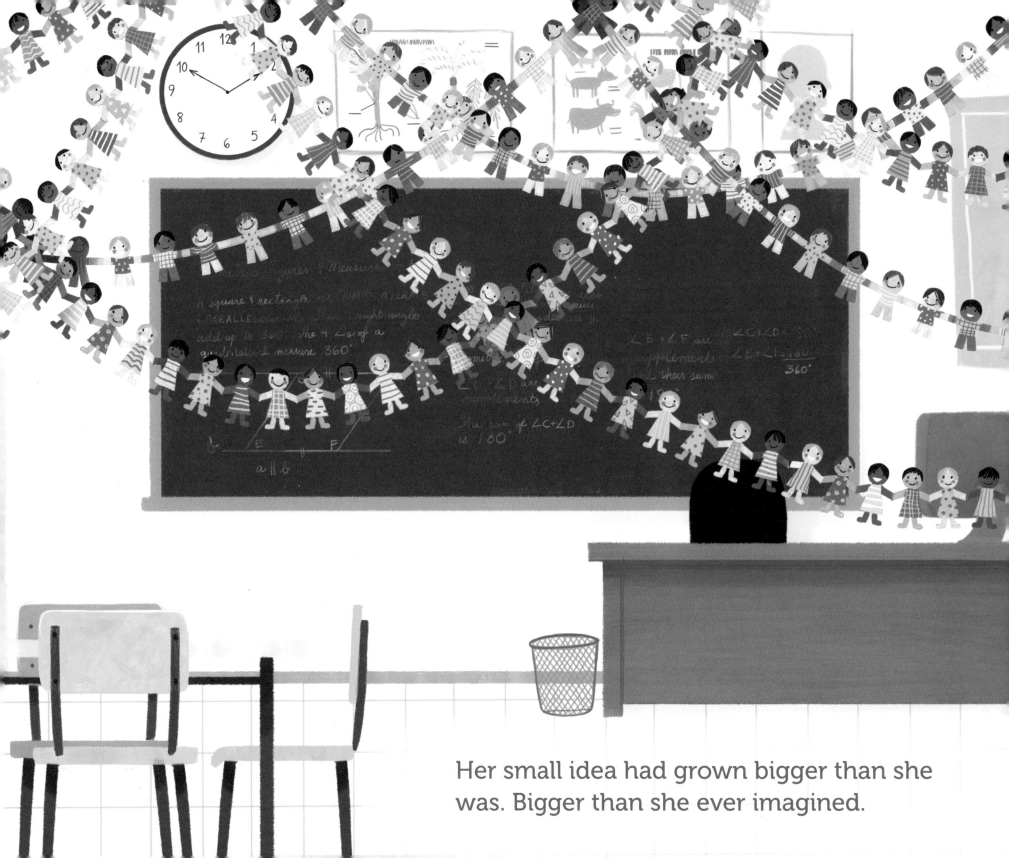

Her small idea had grown bigger than she was. Bigger than she ever imagined.

It was a connection.

Between Luca and Evelyn. Between Annabelle and Nico.

Between Leah and Henry.

And still, Emily's idea grew.

Chains hung in the bakery.

In the hair salon. Even in the post office.

Emily's idea flew from coast to coast . . .
and floated across the ocean.

Friends and strangers joined hands.
Across bridges and town squares.
Beneath subways and bus shelters.

Some people didn't understand.
They ripped. Belittled. Destroyed.

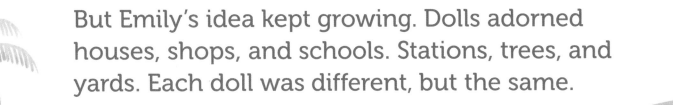

But Emily's idea kept growing. Dolls adorned houses, shops, and schools. Stations, trees, and yards. Each doll was different, but the same.

Emily stuck each story in her scrapbook. Hands holding hands in Japan and Australia. Qatar and Iceland. South Africa and Mexico. Emily felt fluttery. Just like a paper doll in the wind.

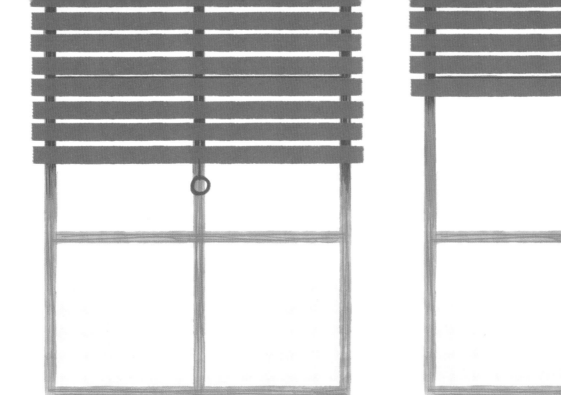
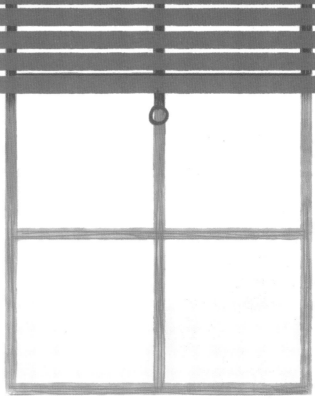

On the last day of school Emily hugged her bulging scrapbook. Ms. Tate had a surprise: a parcel adorned with beautiful stamps.

Emily ripped . . .
Paper dolls cascaded into her lap.
Each doll was different.
But the same.
Just like us.

MAKE YOUR OWN PAPER CHAIN OF DOLLS

You need:
- Paper doll template (see next page)
- Sheets of construction paper (12" x 18") in any color you'd like
- Scissors
- Anything you love to draw with: crayons, pens, pencils, chalk, paint
- Fun things to add details: scraps of patterned paper, old magazines, fabric, envelopes, stamps
- Glue
- Tape

1. Fold one sheet of paper in half lengthwise and cut along the fold. You'll have two strips of paper measuring 6" x 18".

2. Fold one strip of paper in half. Then fold each layer in half again like an accordion.

3. Tear out the doll template page from the back of the book. Cut around the doll shapes.

4. Place a doll template on your folded paper and trace around it on the top layer. Make sure the arms extend past the folds.

5. Use scissors to snip around the template, cutting through all the layers. Make sure you don't cut across the arms so the dolls are holding hands when you unfold the chain.

6. Unfold and let your dolls dance. Now doodle on each doll however you'd like! You can make each doll different, or the same.